Emily
the Stirling Engine

Based on *The Railway Series* by the Rev. W. Awdry

Illustrations by *Robin Davies and Jerry Smith*

EGMONT

EGMONT

We bring stories to life

First published in Great Britain 2005
This edition published in 2013
by Egmont UK Limited
The Yellow Building, 1 Nicholas Road, London W11 4AN

Thomas the Tank Engine & Friends™

CREATED BY BRITT ALLCROFT

HiT entertainment

ISBN 978 1 4052 6969 8
43280/29
Printed in Italy

Stay safe online. Egmont is not responsible for content hosted by third parties.

FSC
MIX
Paper
FSC® C018306

Egmont is passionate about helping to preserve the world's remaining ancient forests.
We only use paper from legal and sustainable forest sources.

This book is made from paper certified by the Forest Stewardship Council® (FSC®),
an organisation dedicated to promoting responsible management of forest resources.
For more information on the FSC, please visit www.fsc.org. To learn more about
Egmont's sustainable paper policy, please visit www.egmont.co.uk/ethical

TO THE TRAINS ⟶

This is a story about Emily the Single Stirling Engine. When she came to the Railway, some of the engines were very unfriendly. But they soon learned that things are not always what they first appear to be . . .

A new engine was arriving on the Island of Sodor.
Thomas puffed happily into Knapford Station.
At the platform, there was a beautiful engine,
with shiny paintwork and gleaming brass fittings.

"Thomas, meet Emily," said The Fat Controller.

"Hello," wheeshed Thomas.

"Hello," puffed Emily.

"Emily, go and collect the coaches, so you can
learn the passenger routes," said The Fat Controller.

"Yes, Sir," smiled Emily, and she steamed away.

The only coaches Emily could find were Annie and Clarabel. Her Driver hooked them up, and Emily puffed slowly and carefully along the track. Annie and Clarabel grumbled all the way.

"There'll be trouble when Thomas finds out," whispered Clarabel.

But Emily couldn't understand why the coaches were so cross. She passed Edward and Percy and whistled a friendly hello. But the engines just stared angrily at her.

Emily was pleased to see Thomas puffing down the line.

"Hello, Thomas!" she called, cheerfully.

But Thomas glared at Emily when he saw she was pulling Annie and Clarabel.

"Those are my coaches!" he muttered, crossly.

Now Thomas was being rude, and Emily had no idea why. She chuffed away, feeling very sad.

Thomas was at Maithwaite Station when The Fat Controller arrived.

"I want you to go to the Docks to pick up some new coaches," he ordered.

"New coaches?" exclaimed Thomas. "But, Sir . . ."

"Really Useful Engines don't argue!" shouted The Fat Controller.

Thomas was very unhappy. He thought the new coaches were for him and he wanted Annie and Clarabel back.

Later that day, Emily returned to the yard. Oliver was very surprised to see her pulling Annie and Clarabel.

"Those are Thomas' coaches!" he cried.

"No wonder he was cross," said Emily. "I will return them straight away."

Meanwhile, Thomas was puffing angrily along the track with the new coaches.

"Don't want new coaches," he chuffed.

Emily was on her way back when a Signalman waved her down. Oliver hadn't cleared his box! Emily sped off to see what was wrong.

Oliver had broken down on the track crossing, and his Driver had gone for help.

Suddenly, Emily heard a whistle in the distance. Thomas was steaming along the track, straight into Oliver. He would never be able to stop in time! Emily quickly charged toward Oliver, and pushed him off the track, just before Thomas rocketed past!

Emily had saved Thomas and Oliver. That evening, The Fat Controller had a special surprise for her.

"Emily, you were a very brave engine!" he said. "So, it gives me great pleasure to present you with two brand new coaches!"

"Thank you, Sir!" replied Emily. "Thomas, I'm sorry I took Annie and Clarabel."

"And I'm sorry I was so cross," said Thomas.

Emily was very happy. She had two beautiful new coaches and a new friend.

Later that summer, The Fat Controller opened some new routes. Emily was given the Flour Mill Special.

"I have to do the Black Loch Run," huffed James.

"He's frightened of the Black Loch Monster," teased Thomas.

"Nonsense!" said James, and he puffed away.

"What's the Black Loch Monster?" asked Emily.

"Nobody knows," said Thomas. "Black shapes move in the water, then disappear."

Emily was glad she didn't have to go to Black Loch.

The next morning, Emily collected the trucks from the flour mill. But they were being naughty. Emily pulled as hard as she could, but the trucks made her go very slowly. Emily was late delivering the flour, so there was no fresh bread that day.

The Fat Controller was cross. "I didn't have any toast for breakfast. If you are late again, you will have to do the Black Loch Run instead of James!"

"I must get the flour to the bakery on time tomorrow!" puffed Emily.

But the next day, the trucks were being naughty again. They told Emily to leave before they were coupled properly, so half of them were left behind.

The Bakery Manager was very angry when Emily arrived with only half the flour. Emily raced back to the mill for the rest of the trucks. She was very cross and shunted them with all her strength. But the trucks had taken their brakes off! They rolled backward and splashed into the duck pond! Emily was covered in a gluey floury mess!

That evening, The Fat Controller came to see her.

"Emily, you are going to take over the Black Loch Run!" he shouted.

"It might be nice," said Thomas, reassuringly.

But Emily wasn't so sure.

The next morning, she puffed sadly to the station. There were lots of excited children and holiday makers waiting for her.

"I mustn't let them down," she thought. And soon Emily was steaming up hills and through valleys.

Finally, Emily reached the murky waters of Black Loch. Suddenly, she saw something move in the water. Her boiler quivered and her valves rattled. Then the water settled, and Emily saw what the monster really was.

"It's a family of seals!" she cried, delightedly.

That evening, Emily took Thomas to watch the seals.

"Black Loch is a nice route after all," said Emily.

"Well, things aren't always what they seem!" said Thomas, cheerfully. And both engines smiled.